PRAISE FOR M[barcode: CH00613640]

Tom Clancy fans open to a strong female lead will clamor for more.

— *DRONE*, PUBLISHERS WEEKLY

Superb! Miranda is utterly compelling!

— *BOOKLIST,* STARRED REVIEW

Miranda Chase continues to astound and charm.

— BARB M.

Escape Rating: A. Five Stars! OMG just start with *Drone* and be prepared for a fantastic binge-read!

— READING REALITY

The best military thriller I've read in a very long time. Love the female characters.

— *DRONE,* SHELDON MCARTHUR, FOUNDER OF THE MYSTERY BOOKSTORE, LA

A fabulous soaring thriller.

— *TAKE OVER AT MIDNIGHT,* MIDWEST BOOK
REVIEW

Meticulously researched, hard-hitting, and suspenseful.

— *PURE HEAT,* PUBLISHERS WEEKLY, STARRED
REVIEW

Expert technical details abound, as do realistic military missions with superb imagery that will have readers feeling as if they are right there in the midst and on the edges of their seats.

— *LIGHT UP THE NIGHT,* RT REVIEWS, 4 1/2
STARS

Buchman has catapulted his way to the top tier of my favorite authors.

— FRESH FICTION

Nonstop action that will keep readers on the edge of their seats.

— *TAKE OVER AT MIDNIGHT,* LIBRARY JOURNAL

M L. Buchman's ability to keep the reader right in the middle of the action is amazing.

— Long and Short Reviews

The only thing you'll ask yourself is, "When does the next one come out?"

— *Wait Until Midnight,* RT Reviews, 4 stars

The first...of (a) stellar, long-running (military) romantic suspense series.

— *The Night is Mine,* Booklist, "The 20 Best Romantic Suspense Novels: Modern Masterpieces"

I knew the books would be good, but I didn't realize how good.

— Night Stalkers series, Kirkus Reviews

Buchman mixes adrenalin-spiking battles and brusque military jargon with a sensitive approach.

— Publishers Weekly

13 times "Top Pick of the Month"

SOUTH POLE RESCUE

AN ANTARCTIC ICE FLIERS ROMANCE STORY

M. L. BUCHMAN

Buchman Bookworks

SIGN UP FOR M. L. BUCHMAN'S NEWSLETTER TODAY

and receive:
Release News
Free Short Stories
a Free Book

Get your free book today. Do it now.
free-book.mlbuchman.com

Other works by M. L. Buchman: *(* - also in audio)*

Action-Adventure Thrillers

Dead Chef
One Chef!
Two Chef!

Miranda Chase
Drone*
Thunderbolt*
Condor*
Ghostrider*
Raider*
Chinook*
Havoc*
White Top*

Romantic Suspense

Delta Force
Target Engaged*
Heart Strike*
Wild Justice*
Midnight Trust*

Firehawks
MAIN FLIGHT
Pure Heat
Full Blaze
Hot Point*
Flash of Fire*
Wild Fire
SMOKEJUMPERS
Wildfire at Dawn*
Wildfire at Larch Creek*
Wildfire on the Skagit*

The Night Stalkers
MAIN FLIGHT
The Night Is Mine
I Own the Dawn
Wait Until Dark
Take Over at Midnight

Light Up the Night
Bring On the Dusk
By Break of Day
AND THE NAVY
Christmas at Steel Beach
Christmas at Peleliu Cove
WHITE HOUSE HOLIDAY
Daniel's Christmas*
Frank's Independence Day*
Peter's Christmas*
Zachary's Christmas*
Roy's Independence Day*
Damien's Christmas*
5E
Target of the Heart
Target Lock on Love
Target of Mine
Target of One's Own

Shadow Force: Psi
At the Slightest Sound*
At the Quietest Word*
At the Merest Glance*
At the Clearest Sensation*

White House Protection Force
Off the Leash*
On Your Mark*
In the Weeds*

Contemporary Romance

Eagle Cove
Return to Eagle Cove
Recipe for Eagle Cove
Longing for Eagle Cove
Keepsake for Eagle Cove

Henderson's Ranch
Nathan's Big Sky*
Big Sky, Loyal Heart*
Big Sky Dog Whisperer*

Other works by M. L. Buchman:

Short Story Series by M. L. Buchman:

ABOUT THIS TITLE

A medical emergency at the South Pole requires immediate evacuation. One problem—it's midwinter and the Pole Station remains cut off for another four months. No one has ever flown to the South Pole in winter.

***Ted Donovan,** the chief pilot of Bernard's Ice Air takes the mission. But if he's going to survive, he needs to take the very best.*

***Jessica Ryan** joined Bernard's as an expert mechanic but always dreamed of flying. When Ted gives her a chance, she leaps in. But her heart never counted on what else she might be flying into.*

FOREWORD

A special shout out to Kenn Borek Air who amazingly achieved the first-ever mid-winter medical evacuation from the Amundsen-Scott South Pole Station from June 14-24, 2016. Two critical patients were safely evacuated at immense risk to the flight crew.

They were deservedly awarded the Michael Collins Trophy, essentially the Nobel Prize of aviation. Prior recipients include: three of the Mars Rover teams, the Hubble telescope team, and the flight crew of US Airways 1549 that managed to land safely in the Hudson River when their plane lost all power on takeoff due to a massive bird strike.

This story would be an impossible fantasy tale—except Kenn Borek Air did it for real when lives were on the line. Many of this story's details are unabashedly lifted from their amazing flight.

1

_____

"FIGHT OR FLIGHT?"

"With you? Easy. Fight," Jessica Ryan shot back. "You challenged, so I get to choose the weapons. Thumb wrestle." She held out her still greasy hand in the proper shape without bothering to wipe it on her coveralls. She was always trying to find a way around Ted Donovan's unbending demeanor. He was maybe three years older than she was, but he'd been the senior pilot at Bernard's Ice Air since shortly after she'd joined five years ago.

"Nope, flight," he jabbed a finger toward *Natasha*, the Twin Otter airplane Jessica had been servicing. "You'll need to load the skis." Had the always proper Ted just teased her?

"Last I checked, it was summer outside." She made a show of peering out the hangar doors, opened wide to Montana June sunshine. "It is! Isn't that amazing."

"Snow skis, Hotshot. Auxiliary tanks, all she'll hold, and full winter gear. Including an emergency camp stocked for two for at least a week. Load both *Boris* and *Natasha*."

She stared out the hangar door again to see if it was lying. It wasn't. It was definitely summer in Montana, it would be July any minute now.

Two birds, spare fuel, skis, and a full emergency kit must mean... "Really?"

"You always were sharp, Hotshot."

"But it's...June!" That load didn't fit a mission onto the Arctic ice. The summer melt was so bad each year now that teams would probably never again be able to walk or sled over the ice to the North Pole. They didn't need maximum fuel tanks to reach anywhere on the Greenland ice cap.

"Worldwide, we're there!" Ted recited BIA's motto.

"That means Antarctica. In the winter? That's *crazy*. No one does that. How far in? McMurdo?"

He just stood there with his arms crossed, looking all handsome and confident, while he waited for her brain to reach the only other possible conclusion.

"Amundsen-Scott? You're flying to the South Pole in the dead of the Southern winter?"

Still he waited, his killer smile on full display.

"Me?"

"Welcome to the game, Hotshot. We're aloft the moment you have our birds ready."

She wanted to let out a Montanan whoop, even if

she was from Seattle. She wanted to hug him, but women didn't randomly hug men like Ted Donovan no matter how pretty he was. For five years she'd been busting her behind, getting every minute of flight time she could, taking every shitty cold-weather assignment she could get, just hoping to come to his attention as a pilot rather than only as a mechanic. Crossing over to pilot was a dream she'd been nurturing for a long, long time.

But saying any of that just wouldn't do.

She managed a totally chill, "Ready in sixty minutes."

The moment his back was turned, she broke into a happy chicken-dance.

"I see that," Ted called out without turning. Blasted man had eyes in the back of his head.

But she did another couple dance steps just to defy him. Ted was flying into the single most impossible airfield on Earth, and he'd just chosen her as his copilot.

Then she turned to look at *Boris*, the second airplane. There was only one reason to take two airplanes to Antarctica in the middle of the southern winter.

Boris would be there...in case *Natasha* crashed and they survived to wait for rescue. A field camp good for a week? That would be enough only if they were very lucky.

2

TED HAD SPOTTED THE REFLECTION OF JESSICA'S DEEP red hair flouncing about in the hangar's office window as she danced.

Damn but that woman cracked him up.

She wasn't his top mechanic, but that was only because Bob had spent his whole life working on these planes. She wasn't his top pilot either, but through pure dint of effort, she soon would be. And what he needed on this flight was both an engineer and a top copilot.

"You're stealing her from me, aren't you? Best damned mechanic to come through here in ages and you're turning her into a driver." Bob greeted him with a growl as he stepped back into the office. The old man sat before a series of charts rolled out across his battered desk—he was completely old school. The edges were tacked down with components of different airplanes.

Ted recognized the blown-out fuel pump head that had almost killed him over Yellowknife in Canada's Northwest Territories. And the steering wheel that was about all that had remained after Davy had augered in a Basler-converted DC-3 during an Alaska wildfire. Davy had delivered his smokejumpers on target, but then had nowhere to put it down except in the dense trees when an engine had seized and the propellor had cut his plane mostly in two.

"You want to fly copilot to the South Pole with me?"

"You think I'm a fucking idiot? You damn well better take the best," he jabbed a finger out the office window at Jessica, "for a bejeezus bonkers stunt like this," he slapped the charts.

Out the window, Ted could see that Jessica had two interns, their supply master, and *Boris'* two pilots on the hustle loading up gear. She'd said sixty minutes, he'd better be ready in forty-five or she just might leave him behind.

Ted leaned in over Bob's shoulder and looked down at the chart.

It was a crazy map. Antarctica was half again bigger than the US, including Alaska. In all that area just four thousand people in high summer—a mere thousand now in dead winter. Forty dots on the entire continent and the surrounding islands had a winter population at all, and only nine of those had more than twenty-five souls in residence.

"The only base within seven hundred miles is summer-only. It's vacant right now. The Russians have a dozen poor souls out at Vostok, but that's eight hundred miles to the wrong side of Amundsen-Scott South Pole Station."

"Real helpful, Bob." Ted hauled over a chair.

Bob had been around since old man Bernard had founded this airline specializing in extremely cold or complex flights. No question Bob had a solution because he always did. He was the one who'd sent him out to prep the Twin Otters as soon as they'd received the call from the US Antarctic Program.

Bob always had a solution.

Ted just had to wait him out sometimes.

Bob aimed a finger at the hangar again. "Twin Otter, it's a primitive bird. Which is a good thing—not a lot to go wrong. Other than the engines and flaps, she's almost all mechanical. No other hydraulics to freeze up on you."

"That's why you didn't select the DC-3's." The Twin Otter was an unlikely bird to fly halfway around the world and stage a daring medevac. Twin turboprop engines with big three-bladed propellors on a high wing, she could carry nineteen passengers or nine thousand pounds of cargo and fuel. This time it would be crew, a single patient, and all the rest fuel. And even that would be marginal. The South Pole was a long way from everywhere.

"Right. Too many systems to keep warm to make the run in a DC-3. You're going to be flying right near the freezing temperature of jet fuel. Even the specialized AN8 fuel turns to glue at minus seventy-five Fahrenheit. Hydraulic oil might as well be a solid by then. That's why the Air National Guard can't fly their LC-130 Hercules Skibirds in. The moment they land, they'd turn into a popsicle and lie there until spring—if they didn't freeze solid on the flight down."

"How high do I have to climb?"

"You can't. You have to stay low. Temperature drops as you climb into higher altitude. If the ground is at minus seventy, any altitude is gonna freeze your ass and you drop like a brick. The ground there is at ninety-three hundred feet above sea level. You keep your ass under eleven. Down at ten thou is better."

"Christ, Bob. You want me to fly into unknown territory at five hundred feet above the ground? And there's no easy way to visually gauge elevation over ice and snow, white on white. No reference point."

"It gets better."

"How is that possible?"

"It's winter," Bob was definitely enjoying something, but Ted couldn't see what.

"Yeah, cold. I get it."

"Not just," Jessica interrupted, bouncing on her toes in the doorway as if she had too much energy to keep it all inside. "It'll be pitch dark the whole way from the Antarctic Circle."

Ted groaned. He hadn't thought that far ahead yet.

Then Jessica grinned at him. "Unless the Aurora Australis is kicking off."

3

JESSICA FLEW THE FIRST LEG FROM THE COPILOT'S SEAT. There wasn't a moment for idle chatter, Ted remained immersed in planning for the entire flight.

A full load of fuel in the standard tanks covered nine hundred miles. The built-in extended-range tanks added another two hundred miles with a total of four hundred and seventy gallons. And the auxiliary bladder tank the interns had rigged in the center of the cargo bay after pulling out most of the seats, would hold another two hundred and fifty gallons. It would let them fly the final leg of one thousand, five hundred, and fifty-two miles to the South Pole with a ten-percent reserve.

That was the last leg. This first leg was easy.

They were aloft in *Natasha* out of Missoula, Montana forty minutes after they received the call. The backup crew flew *Boris* off their right wing under the mid-morning sunshine. Other than a brief rain squall at the Wyoming-Colorado border, the flight to Texas was uneventful.

Most of the flight was spent discussing every step of the logistics over the intercom. Ted let her fly most of it as he was constantly on the radio to *Boris'* pilots or checking some detail by phone with Bob back at Bernard's Ice Air.

They would only be flying the first and last two legs themselves: Missoula to Texas, then southern Chile to the Antarctic Peninsula, and on to the Pole.

After Texas, she, Ted, and *Boris'* crew wouldn't see the planes again until the southern tip of Chile. Meanwhile, multiple crews would hopscotch the small planes south with refueling stops in Costa Rica, Peru, Central Chile, and finally at Punta Arenas, Chile—the kick-off point for Antarctica—with the briefest stops possible. There better not be any other crises, most of BIA's pilots were involved in just the first hours of the rescue—ten full crews of pilots and copilots were needed to move the planes south this fast.

Her and Ted's job was to be fresh and rested by the time *Boris* and *Natasha* were delivered. Even by jet with the best connections, Texas to southern Chile was going to take them twenty hours and three stops from Austin. No such thing as a direct flight where they were going.

"Business class?" Jessica asked as they slid into the luxurious side-by-side seats on the Boeing 737.

"If the flights had First Class, I'd have gotten it, but the hops are too short. We need to get as much sleep as we can."

Sleep? There was no chance of Jessica falling asleep. Her excitement high had slid most of the way back to normal as the grim realities of this flight had been discussed. But even when deadheading like this, the pilot in her just couldn't let go enough to sleep. "It's five in the afternoon," was the best excuse she could come up with.

"Maybe we can sleep in Chile once we get there," Ted's sigh was one of the first indicators that he was human.

"What, Mister Super-pilot can't sleep on airplanes either?"

"Not a wink," he actually winked at her as if to belie his point. "Mom says even as a baby I'd be quiet but wide-eyed for the entire flight, then have a fit when they carried me off the plane."

"Bet you were a handful."

"Nah! Mom said I was a good kid, except when I had to leave an airplane. I would wager that you were though."

"Totally! Thankfully, I got my red hair from Mom. She understood, though she always griped about how paybacks were hell." They'd also been so close that her loss was still a hole in Jessica's heart.

"Sorry," Ted read her face far too easily as the plane

backed out of the gate and began taxiing, "I didn't know she was dead. How did it happen?"

"Her new boyfriend got her started on bicycling. She really got into it. Big charity rides, weekend bike camping, cycle commuting, the whole bit. A drunk clipped her when he ran a red light. She never stood a chance." Jessica did her best to shrug it off. Six years hadn't eased the loss. The month of brain-dead coma before she could bring herself to pull the plug was something she wouldn't be sharing anytime soon.

Mom's boyfriend had been a good guy. Even offered to stand with her when they disconnected Mom, but she hadn't trusted what she might say. It had turned out to be a good call—if she'd had a target that day, she'd have beaten herself bloody against it.

"Well, she'd be damn proud of you if she could see you now." Ted actually rested his hand on hers as the engines roared to life and they began the takeoff roll down the runway.

Jessica held on to his strength as the power of the twin turbofans hurtled them down the runway and aloft.

"Mom and I always held hands for this part." Her voice felt like it had cracked out of her chest.

"Was she afraid of flying?"

"No, she loved it. *We* loved it. She always watched the Internet for those last-minute deals where they're trying to fill seats at any price. Every month or so I'd get out of school on a Friday and she'd meet me with our knapsacks already packed. 'Doing your homework in Chicago this weekend.' Or Pittsburgh, Phoenix, Nashville. It didn't matter, she always made it an adventure. Back in time for school Monday, typically straight off a redeye flight. They were the best weekends of my life. I always loved flying."

"Then why a mechanic and not a pilot?"

"Cheaper. I could get a job faster if I got my A&P license. Airframe and powerplant engineers lack the glory, but we get paid well. We never had a lot of money, but Mom sure knew how to enjoy life."

4

TED WONDERED WHEN HE'D LOST THAT, IF HE'D EVER had it.

He *liked* his life—other than the blood-ugly divorce he'd never think about again. But he'd certainly never done a happy dance at being chosen to fly. Thrilled, excited, sometimes afraid? Sure. So joyously happy that he couldn't hold it in as Jessica had demonstrated on the hangar floor? Not even when he'd banged out his first-ever double with bases loaded in Little League.

The joy simply poured from Jessica. He could feel the fire of it as she continued to squeeze his hand while the plane climbed to cruising altitude.

He did his best not to draw her attention to it, but she eventually noticed and let go.

She blushed until her fair skin was almost the color of her hair.

"Now you're going to have to explain that."

"What?" But pressing her fingers to her cheeks said that she knew exactly what he'd meant.

"I've seen you grab onto someone in the hangar when you're happy with them or laughing at some joke they just told." And he'd done his best not to envy them that easy familiarity. That was a gift he'd never had.

"That's normal people. Not you, Mr. Senior Pilot."

"Am I so untouchable?"

"Yes," she gasped it out in a small voice.

He wasn't quite ready to ask what she meant by that.

He was only a few years older than her, so that wasn't it. Bernard Ice Air's first-generation of pilots had run the operation themselves for years. But when one retired from flight, the others had followed quickly. They ran the place now, and he'd simply been the senior-most of the next generation. Not the oldest, but he'd taken to flight much the way Jessica had these last five years since Bob had hired her.

There wasn't a type of aircraft that BIA flew that Ted didn't certify himself in during his first year. He took every flight they'd give him, even the routine drudge flights no one else wanted. Ice and snow survival classes—he never missed a one. He'd sat for endless hours just listening to the senior pilots talk about this landing or that crash. He'd racked up the hours and experience until he'd been their obvious pick for chief pilot. Maybe he had been a little too focused on his career.

Jessica had done much the same since coming on board. He couldn't seem to turn around but there she was listening, learning, absorbing anything anyone said. He'd quietly fed a lot of flights her way and she'd thrived on them. Yet she exuded life while he...merely lived it?

"There's a lot to like about you, Jessica."

"There is? I always thought I was more a pain-in-the-ass type."

He couldn't help laughing. "I've certainly been told that enough times about you."

"You have? Shit! I'm sorry. I never meant—"

Ted rested his hand on hers again to stop her.

She stared down at his hand, so he pulled it back.

"It's usually accompanied by a comment about your tenacity until you learn everything about whatever it is. I have that same need. It's how I got to my, ahem, *lofty* position."

"Hard to imagine the Great Chief Pilot being a PIA."

"Just ask any of the management guys."

She didn't quite look up at him. "There's a lot I like about you too." Then she determinedly turned to stare out the window.

Their first hop was just across the width of Texas

and their conversation had been slow enough that they were already descending.

She didn't take his hand for the landing.

But he hoped she would on the next takeoff.

5

Jessica was absolutely losing her mind.

Four flights sitting far too close to Ted Donovan was causing strange reactions that she couldn't quite anchor to any part of her body.

It definitely wasn't her mind because she was rapidly losing that. Maybe she was getting too little oxygen. Thinking thoughts about Ted Donovan as anything other than BIA's chief pilot was simply too bizarre for reality.

She considered switching seats with one of the other pilots from *Boris*' flight crew—also making the leap ahead with them—but didn't want to move away from Ted either.

On each flight, he'd subtly offered his hand. She hadn't taken it out of Houston or Bogotá, Colombia. For both of those long flights she'd pretended that she didn't see the gesture.

But since neither of them were inclined to sleep on the pair of five-hour flights, they had talked. For the Houston to Bogotá leg, she'd carefully kept it professional. Ted was soon drawing diagrams to explain the quirks of handling BIA's various aircraft during extreme conditions. She, in turn, found he was equally interested in the esoterica of airframe and powerplant maintenance—"After all, my life depends on what you do there."

But for the Bogotá to Santiago, Chile leg, they were both tired enough to just talk. They'd slowly shifted three time zones eastward as they traveled south, but that didn't stop it being the middle of the night Montana time. No, it made it worse, as her watch kept reporting it was later and later with each time zone. Actually earlier and earlier because they'd left midnight behind somewhere over Ecuador and it was now the next day. That wasn't right either. Earlier and later? Two a.m., three a.m., in...some time zone.

Whenever they were, her defenses around Ted Donovan were shutting down one by one, even though she wasn't running any checklist she could think of.

He asked more questions about her mother, bringing back so many good memories that it was hard not to weep her thanks out on his shoulder. Mom's ending had been bad and Jessica had shut down *all* memories to leave that behind. But the good parts had been *so* good. Even during the rebellious teen years —"my red-headed years, Mom had always called them"—there'd been far more good than bad. Her first real heartbreak hadn't sent her to her best friend, it had sent her to Mom. He gave those memories back to her.

In turn, Ted had told her about a childhood so normal compared to hers that it was hard to credit. Two parents, older brother, kid sports, school, chasing girls, baseball team captain at his small Montana school. A short marriage and a divorce that he dropped after just that many words. He looked as grim as she'd felt about Mom's death, so she didn't ask.

"Besides, I'd always known I was meant to fly. I shoveled a lot of winter sidewalks and even more manure in horse barns to pay for my lessons. I also didn't waste my time with any other outfits," he teased her. "I was hanging out at the BIA hangar before I even had my private ticket."

"Wasting—" she put on her best offended tone for him. "I was a working mechanic at Harbour Air in Seattle by the time I was eighteen and licensed before I was twenty, I'll have you know."

"Which explains exactly why Bob hired you." He was right. There wasn't a better match than Twin Otter planes with water pontoons to Twin Otter planes with snow skis. Salt water to ice cold. Those were just details, big important details, but details. As if her career had been headed straight to BIA before she'd ever heard of them. She'd certainly applied the day she had.

When he offered his hand after the layover and fast airport breakfast of *huevos con jamón,* which sounded much better than the runny eggs and slab of hyper-salty ham they'd been served, she took it without thinking, though they hadn't even left the gate yet.

She fell asleep while they were still taxiing.

6

TED WASN'T SURE QUITE WHERE TO LOOK.

He simply put his arm on the armrest and she'd taken his hand as if it was the most natural thing in the world. His skin wasn't particularly dark, just a good summer tan, but her fingers appeared alabaster in comparison. They were fine, but the grime under ragged short nails showed she used them hard.

He looked at her face just as her eyes slid shut.

The turn onto the active runway caused her to tip her head onto his shoulder.

He wanted to wake her up and tease her about "I never sleep on a plane." Yet he wanted her head to remain on his shoulder forever.

It wasn't until they'd climbed all of the way up to cruising altitude that he dared rest his cheek on her hair. Soft as a breath on his cheek, it was smooth and silky as the wind over a perfectly formed airplane wing.

Jessica Ryan. Asleep on his shoulder.

Just enjoy the moment and don't read anything into it, boy.

But he wanted to, which was a surprise.

It had been a long time since *that* had happened.

7

PUNTA ARENAS WAS THE JUMPING OFF POINT FOR FORTY-six of the seventy bases on the Antarctic continent and islands. But that was in the southern summer. In the winter, the southernmost city in the world was a ghost town—a ghost town of a hundred thousand residents, but still incredibly quiet in the off season. Not only were there no Antarctic flights, there were few research vessels and no tourist cruise ships either. The city's heyday as a coaling station for interoceanic commerce had died long ago with the opening of the Panama Canal.

None of that mattered.

They'd beaten the Twin Otter's arrival in Punta Arenas, Chile, by twelve hours.

The three hours of sleep on that final flight hadn't been enough by far, and Jessica hadn't given it another thought when she'd crashed into one of their hotel room's two queen beds for a straight eight.

But it had been a galvanic shock when she'd woken to hear Ted Donovan taking a shower. She'd feigned sleep until he was done and out of the room before hurrying through her own shower.

He'd left a note: *Meet you in restaurant downstairs for breakfast.*

They'd landed at six p.m., slept until two a.m., and met in the restaurant by three. They were the only people there. Thankfully, the hotel had left the coffee on and a pile of day-old muffins. They also had a hot water tap and packets of hot chocolate which was a nice surprise.

Scott-Amundsen was reporting the patient in non-stable critical condition. Should they try to carry a doctor or a med-tech? He or she would weigh as much as thirty gallons of fuel. The fifty-five fewer miles of range could become critical if they struck a bad headwind.

Their best calculations estimated that a thirty-knot headwind would tap all of their reserve, and thirty-one knots would force them to land on the untested ice before they reached the station. That thirty-mile-an-hour winds were their safety limit—and winds of seventy or even a hundred miles per hour were common during the South Pole winter—was...worrisome.

Basically, it was scaring the crap out of her.

Ted, of course, had remained perfectly calm as they'd verified each other's calculations on that crucial point.

It was presently blowing fifteen knots at Rothera Station—the British base they'd be staging from on the Antarctic Peninsula—and twenty-two at the Pole. It didn't get much more favorable than that. Except there were no winter weather stations anywhere in the fifteen hundred miles between the two.

"That's Seattle to Austin, Texas, with no idea of what's going on in between. You could squeeze a whole hurricane in that gap and never know."

"Except it's a sea of ice and hurricanes are tropical." Ted was always so literal.

"The vasty nothingness," Jessica was just glad to be avoiding any discussion of last night. As the last flight had landed, she'd woken on Ted's shoulder like it was the Rock of Gibraltar, so safe and solid. He too slept with his cheek upon her hair. How was that even possible?

"The great unknown," Ted agreed, looking at the blank expanse on the chart. He also wasn't mentioning last night—Thank God. Or was he? Were they the "great unknown" or was she doing her usual overthinking the crap out of everything? Overthinking. Definitely. Hopefully?

"The planes will be here in about three more hours." And if it was *not* "Thank God?" Ted was a wonderfully comfortable man to be around once she got past the senior pilot role that he wore like a knight's armor.

But they worked together.

There was no way talking about sleeping against each other while holding hands was going to be an easy or comfortable conversation. Of course, since when had she listened to common sense?

Ted looked as if he too was about to change the subject to last night when the *Boris* flight crew wandered in as bleary eyed as she felt.

After that, it was pure business.

It wasn't until her second cup of hot chocolate that she noticed the light pressure of his knee against hers.

He moved it away at her flinch of surprise.

Sticking to her habit of pursuing stupid ideas, she tipped her knee back into his.

It was insane. She was a grown woman playing footsie...kneesie...with her company's senior pilot under a hotel lobby table in southern Chile before flying to Antarctica.

Mom wouldn't have loved it. She would have wondered why Jessica was making up such a crazy story.

Except the pressure of Ted's knee against hers was undeniably real.

8

THE PLANES ARRIVED AT SIX A.M., THREE HOURS TO dawn. Punta Arenas only enjoyed seven hours of daylight this time of year. Far more than they'd find to the south. Rothera would have twilight only, but the South Pole would be pitch dark twenty-four hours a day.

Ted tried to help, but Jessica was doing such an I'm-a-force-of-nature-so-look-out mechanic's inspection that he decided it was safer to stay out of her way, file his flight plan, and get a last-minute weather update.

The planes had just been flown forty-two hours straight through, by five different pairs of pilots. Jessica was mounting the snow skis around the wheels, stripping out every extra ounce of weight like removing the seat they'd tentatively planned for the med tech they'd decided against (Jessica would use the satellite radio to be talked through needed care, if it wasn't too awful), checking over every element of the plane, and making sure the fuel was loaded with plenty of reserve to reach their first stop at Rothera.

She was somehow everywhere at once. The copilot from the *Boris* team tried to keep up, he really did, but he was a pilot first and second and a mechanic only as a distant third. He never stood a chance.

In under an hour of whirlwind activity, Jessica had both planes ready. Ted was in the pilot's seat and heading aloft almost without being aware of how he'd gotten there. The two pilots sitting in *Boris* looked equally shocked.

The five-hour flight into the descending darkness left little time for talk. There was a hard blow kicking over the Drake Passage, generally rated as the most dangerous water in the world.

"Wave reports over forty feet, Ted. So no water landings today, okay?" Her voice over the headset intercom made it feel as if she was whispering in his ear.

"Yes, ma'am, Jessica, ma'am. It wasn't on my filed flight plan anyway."

She navigated him around the worst of the weather, but they were riding the twilight south. They were aloft out of Punta Arenas well before sunrise and even though they were flying through the morning and landing at high noon in Rothera, they never quite saw the sun. It remained out of sight, casting a dusky twilight—brilliant with reds skittering through the broken clouds.

"Red in the morning," she said softly over the intercom.

"Sailors take warning. Good thing we're flying."

"Good thing." Jessica repeated. She sounded as if she was testing the feeling of those words far more than she was agreeing with anything.

He could still feel the spot on his knee where they'd brushed together under the breakfast table. How ridiculously sappy was that?

"It's a surprisingly mild ten degrees Fahrenheit at Rothera," she announced as if they hadn't both read the same report an hour ago.

"Milder than a Montana winter. Hardly worth worrying about."

She made a thoughtful noise, then rerouted him around another squall line.

As much as he wanted to know what Jessica was thinking, he couldn't bring himself to ask. Because if he did, she'd ask what he was thinking, and he'd be damned if he knew.

Waking to see her sprawled out, asleep on the bed next to his, her long hair completely hiding her face beneath soft waves... Well, it was a hell of a nice sight to wake up to, he'd give it that.

9

ROTHERA WAS UNREMARKABLE IN THAT JESSICA WAS conscious for so little time there. The British base had just twenty-two winter residents down from a hundred and thirty in the summer. In winter it was the sixth largest population below the Antarctic Circle. In the summer it rose to third, behind only McMurdo and the South Pole.

After a white-knuckle-rough five-hour passage that had sapped their strength, they had a mandatory rest layover of eight hours. Once she'd made sure that both planes were fueled to their very limits with AN8 fuel, she crashed into a bed again. Thankfully, she had her own bunkroom, so she didn't need to think about Ted Donovan sleeping just the other side of the wall.

Or she didn't have to think about him much, because exhaustion took over and she was asleep again.

Now it was all about the weather.

Mid-June and below the Antarctic Circle meant the time of day was fairly meaningless. The fast travel had left her so jetlagged that the time was even more meaningless. She'd slept, she was awake, and she was about to embark on a flight as crazy as Lindbergh crossing the Atlantic or Byrd's first-ever flight over the South Pole.

She tried to remind herself that Admiral Byrd had made his flight in a 1929 Ford Trimotor. To reach the heights of the Polar Plateau, Byrd had littered Antarctica with empty gas tanks and dumped their emergency equipment. He'd also done it in the constant November sunlight across eight hundred and fifty miles from McMurdo.

In contrast, they'd be flying in the dead of night for fifteen hundred miles from Rothera to the Pole because there was no practical way to reach McMurdo —it was far beyond where the Twin Otter's fuel could go. Even if they could get to New Zealand in the first place, all the fuel she could load wouldn't get them across the wide Southern Ocean from there to McMurdo Station.

It was eight p.m. at Rothera when they departed in *Natasha*. The winds were favorable, and the South Pole was reporting a temperature of only minus seventy, which was five degrees above where their fuel would freeze. The *Boris* crew saw them off. They'd be ready if she and Ted crashed in *Natasha*. She could only hope it was enough because there was no one else who could come get them before spring. Suddenly that one week of emergency supplies she'd barely resisted winnowing to save weight looked painfully undersized.

All twenty-two of the Brits came out for their departure as well. It was easy to guess why.

"You made friends for life with that maneuver," she teased Ted as they slid down the ice runway and rotated aloft.

"Me? I didn't do anything special." He'd sent the crews who had ferried the planes to southern Chile to clear out the fruit-and-vegetable section at the Punta Arenas market while she'd readied the planes. The planes had plenty of excess capacity for the Drake Passage crossing, so he'd delivered over five hundred pounds of "freshies" *in the dead of winter.* She wouldn't be surprised if he'd received several marriage proposals for that stunt.

"You were married—" It slipped out before she could stop it as they climbed over the spine of the Trans-Antarctic Mountains before turning south over the Larsen Ice Shelf and the Weddell Sea.

"I was." His acid tone told her to drop it, but now it hung between them in the darkness lit only by the LCDs of the instrument panel. There was nothing to see out the window. The crescent moon wouldn't rise until after they'd already reached the Pole. There was just the burning sweep of the stars and their readouts. Not even a pretty Aurora to provide a distraction.

She tried to concentrate on their route. They'd climbed to ten thousand feet. They'd be more efficient up at the aircraft's twenty-five-thousand-foot ceiling of operation, but the air up there would be fifty degrees colder than it was here and their gas would freeze.

They were well out over the Weddell Sea and most of the way to the Ronne Ice Shelf before he answered.

"She was a needy, passive-aggressive, master of manipulation. I never saw it coming. Got me so damn twisted up that I thought it was all my fault when she started cheating. Took the goddamn lawyer almost slapping me up side the head for me to see it. How lame is that?"

"Pretty lame."

He twisted to look at her in surprise.

Maybe she should have taken the more diplomatic route but that wasn't her. "I mean having to have a lawyer do it. No best friend to straighten you out?"

"That's who she was cheating with."

She cringed. "Okay, so...can we just write my question off to foot-in-mouth disease?"

"Or to my being a total idiot?"

"There's a noun that shouldn't ever be allowed in the presence of the great Ted Donovan. I think it's more that you're a genuinely nice guy."

"Yeah, and look what that got me."

Jessica buried herself in recalculating the fuel, something she planned to do every half hour for the entire flight down and back. Though it had only been twenty minutes since her last check.

What had it gotten him? It had made her really hope that Ted's attraction to her was more than just proximity on a long mission. That it might even match her attraction to him which, she knew, had started the day she'd walked into the Bernard Ice Air hangar for the very first time.

He'd been married then. And whatever his wife had done to him, he'd never shown it for an instant at work. One day he was talking about needing to be home for dinner...and the next day he wasn't. That had been the only change. Word of the divorce had swept through the outfit, but always in quiet whispers and never when he was around.

He'd also never shown his attraction to her, until she'd taken his hand on that first takeoff. Or had he taken hers? She flexed her fingers and couldn't even remember.

There's a lot to like about you, Jessica.

But was there enough?

10

TED THANKED THE BRILLIANT STARS THAT THE FLIGHT TO the Pole passed without event.

Sections of the Polar Plateau along their route rose over ten thousand feet, but Jessica's calculations gave him permission to climb as high as eleven based on the ambient air temperature—so plowing sight-unseen into the ice was no longer a worry.

She ran the deicing equipment like a woman conducting an orchestra. Never too much or too little. The ice buildup on the wing, tail, and propellor surfaces were monitored by calculating airspeed versus fuel burn rates.

The wing boots were run through inflate-deflate cycles whenever she wasn't happy with the numbers. The leading edges of the wings and rear stabilizer had been replaced with expandable rubber boots. By inflating them, it cracked the built-up ice, which then blew away. But it couldn't be left too long or the boot might not be able to break it up if the ice was building quickly. Do it too often and a thin sheen of flexible ice would built up and then not crack free.

Heating elements had been placed along the propellor blades to melt any ice. But they couldn't be left on all the time either. There were power drains and re-icing issues there. Between that and the navigation, there was plenty to keep Jessica fully occupied.

Or at least any lesser person.

He expected that Jessica still had plenty of bandwidth because she was Jessica.

"Don't you ever stop being amazing?"

"Me?" She blurted out in surprise. His ex had been all about careful words and controlled emotions. Jessica had about as much delicate artifice as a bulldozer.

"Yes, you."

"I'm not amazing. I'm just me."

"Yeah, and look what that's gotten *you*." She had so much.

"Like what?"

He could only laugh. "You're BIA's only A&P mechanic who is also a fully certified pilot. Not just to FAA standards, to our standards. You've been to so many places that it makes my head spin. I'm Missoula born and bred. Didn't stick my nose outside the Front Range but once or twice a year to visit the grandparents until BIA sent me there. You dance for the pure joy of being happy. That's a gift and half right there."

"Most people laugh at me when I do that."

"I bet a lot more are laughing *with* you than you think. Or wishing they could be like you."

"You don't ever do a happy dance?"

"Haven't yet."

"That's sad, Ted. If you aren't celebrating life, are you actually living it? Mom used to say that all the time and I think it's true."

Ted kept an eye on their drift rate. They had a rear quartering wind trying to shove them sideways. It wasn't too hard, but he had to keep an eye on it. That wind was helping them now, but it would be a headwind on the return flight when they were traveling back with a patient aboard.

And there it was again. He'd enjoyed his life, except for his three years of servitude with his ex, but he'd never celebrated it.

Jessica seemed to celebrate it with every breath. What would it take to do that?

11

JESSICA WAS THE FIRST TO SPOT THE GLOW ON THE horizon.

After seven full hours of darkness, it was a shock.

"The moon won't be up for hours."

Ted laughed but didn't explain.

"Did they turn on all of the station lights for us?"

"Good guess, but no."

She kept her mouth shut and waited. Ted Donovan was known as a real straight shooter, but he was teasing her. She was sure of it. Ever since that moment in the hangar he wouldn't let go of, when he'd caught her dancing. He'd never teased anyone at work even a little that she'd ever heard.

The packed snow of Jack F. Paulus Skiway didn't have an instrument landing system. And because the ice was on the move even here in the center of the continent, GPS wasn't all it could be as a reference.

Jessica saw the light bloom out of the darkness. "It's like magic."

"It's more like oil drums," Ted was laughing.

And that's exactly what it was. A line of oil drums had been partly filled with jet fuel and lit off. A dozen drums down the length of the runway's edge.

"But it *is* like magic. A fairy tale city." Each fire drum lit a great circle of the ice, making the white shine and flicker with a happy orange glow. At the far end of the runway, the main building was indeed well lit. It might be four a.m. on Chile and Rothera Station time, but the South Pole Station was most connected to McMurdo and New Zealand—at least for four months of the summer when flights could make this passage with some semblance of safety—so they set their clocks to match. Here it was just eight in the evening.

At the far end of the runway, she had Ted pause but not shut down. Then, just as she'd instructed, three people ran out and shoved big wooden boards against the leading edge of the skis before backing away.

"Let's do it."

"Oh, you are so good." Ted ran the throttles back up, easing them onto the wood before shutting down.

"I am, aren't I?" Now their skis wouldn't freeze to the ice.

They'd made it to the South Pole, in the dead of winter, with a full hour-and-a-quarter fuel reserve. They wouldn't be nearly so lucky going back. That headwind had her worried.

12

"Well, that was a big hit."

"I'm a winning sort of guy." He'd held back one patient's-weight of "freshies" from what he'd given to Rothera. Two hundred pounds of oranges, apples, bananas...the winterovers had gone wild.

Now it was just the two of them. He'd brought Jessica out to see the South Pole marker. Not the ceremonial one at the front of the station where a reflective sphere had been placed atop a candy-striped pole. They were at the real marker that showed how far the ice had drifted since the first one was placed.

It was a quiet corner of the world, close by the station building but also very separate. The two-story structure was mounted atop massive pillars to keep it clear of the snow. A few kilometers to the left was the South Pole Telescope. Ten kilometers to the right was an under-ice seismometer station. Straight ahead there was nothing for thousands of miles other than the tiny Russian station at the geo-magnetic South Pole.

"The silence is astonishing."

Ted listened. After all the hours on jets and in the Twin Otter, the silence made his ears ring. The only sounds were the slick sounds when he moved inside his heavy parka and the wind slid ice crystals along the surface.

"It's like I can hear the world breathing."

"Well, it's certainly moving. We're standing on nine thousand feet of ice drifting sideways at ten meters a year." Which was still impossibly strange, though he'd been here several times before.

"Nine kajillion stars sparkling in the heavens." Her hood was tilted back as she stared up at the sky.

And there were, but all he could see was Jessica. Well, the outline of her massive orange parka etched in the darkness. It was minus sixty-seven on the ground, and the wind chill supposedly made it minus ninety-two—it felt colder.

"You know what night this is?"

He didn't.

"June twenty-fourth, the traditional mid-summer's eve. A night of mystery and magic if Shakespeare is to be believed."

"It is a beautiful sight even if it *is* freezing. Your first trip to the South Pole, I had to show you the true pole. Every direction is north from here."

She made a show of running a small circle around

the marker, then pumped both arms aloft. "She did it, folks. She ran around the world!"

For once he didn't think. He didn't plan.

He just pulled her in and pushed the front of their hoods together until their faces were in a tiny shared cocoon of warmth. He hesitated when their lips were just a breath apart.

She didn't.

With the thick layers they each wore, their arms were far from clasping around each other, but that did nothing to diminish the kiss. Locking lips with Jessica Ryan was like kissing summer in the middle of winter. Which was such an appropriate metaphor that he smiled.

She smiled back.

And soon they were both laughing.

"You just wanted to kiss a girl at the South Pole."

"I just wanted to kiss *you* wherever I could."

"Let's go inside and try this again. Or else."

"Or else what?" Would he ever keep up with this woman?

"Or else the tips of our noses will freeze together."

13

THEY'D SLEPT.

It *was* the main purpose of the layover at the South Pole. Their plane didn't want to sit for twelve hours and slowly turn into a block of ice. But even with two pilots, fifteen hours of continuous flight over such difficult terrain—Rothera to the Pole and back—was an unacceptable risk. They had to take a break.

They hadn't made love, but they'd certainly snuggled and finally slept spooned together on her bunk, both holding tight.

Oh, Jessica wished she could hold onto this moment forever. She'd always found the bright side of whatever life threw at her, but it was rare for life to throw something so perfect that she doubted its truth.

That niggling set of nerves woke her while Ted slept on. She slithered free.

She wasn't able to watch him for long, having him

in her bed was simply too...something. Odd? Peculiar? Fantastic? A possession by space aliens arriving at the South Pole and replacing them with pod people?

Instead, she'd gone outside to meet the South Pole crew. They'd worked for days out in the brutal cold and wind fashioning that skiway for them out of the drifting snow. Now they had to prepare her plane to takeoff again. That would take two or three hours.

They attached big hot-air blowers to each engine, but kept them on low. If the metal heated too unevenly, it could crack a fan blade and then they'd be stuck for the winter. Being stuck here with Ted Donovan for the next four months wasn't the worst idea she'd ever heard. Being stuck here with Ted and a patient dying in the station's infirmary, that wasn't a possibility. The doc had at least said he was stable enough for transport—barely.

A third heater was eased into the cargo bay, but that had to be run even lower. It would be all too easy to shatter a windshield with a big blast of heat inside and minus seventy outside the thin piece of glass.

A snow-tracked fuel truck drove up beside her plane and pumped it full of AN8 fuel. She checked carefully to make sure that the sluggish liquid was topped up to the limit of every tank: wings, long-range, and the bladder that lumped in the center of the cabin.

That only left—

"We have a problem."

She whirled to see Ted close behind her. "If that's

your idea of a morning-after greeting, we need to have a long talk."

Jessica barely had time to gasp in surprise before he had her pinned against the side of the fuselage and was kissing the daylights out of her. Except there was no daylight here. She kissed him back until she saw stars. There were plenty of stars here.

"That'll have to do for now. We have a problem."

Smug. Ted sounded deeply smug. For herself, she was still a bit star-dazzled. "Are you going to tell me, or is this twenty questions?"

"The doc says that the first patient is stable enough that we should be okay."

"I know. I asked too. Wait a sec... *First* patient?"

"Girl is quick," Ted replied. "We have an *optional* second patient to transport. Our call. Macular degeneration, they're going blind. They need to retreat to a lower altitude and get treatment."

"Yes."

"It's not that simple. Fuel, headwinds, nowhere to refuel in fifteen hundred miles."

"Fifteen hundred and fifty-two. But the answer is yes. Now go get them ready while I figure out how we're going to do that."

Even through his parka, she could read his brief amusement. Then he stroked a gloved finger down the side of her hood as if he was brushing her cheek underneath. He'd already made his choice, but he wasn't going to force it if she deemed it was unsafe.

Without a further word, he hustled back toward the station building.

She paced once around the plane. The DHC-6 Twin Otter was the pickup truck of airplanes. It even sounded like one when you were slamming the pilots' doors shut—which was the only reliable way to get them to latch. There was a reason there had been a thousand of these built and most were still going strong. The airframe wasn't some sleek little pretty thing. It was tough and robust. She knew every inch of how true that was from the inside and the pilot-side.

She stepped up to the head of the heater crew. "How long did you make the skiway?"

"We took your maximum takeoff run of twelve hundred feet and doubled it. You have twenty-four hundred feet out there."

"How long would it take to make it three thousand?"

"Well, out past the end wasn't too rugged. The worst of the drifting was here, near the station."

"Even a rough pack would do. I'm hoping we're light on the skis by then but we'll need room to abort if there's a problem."

He looked out into the darkness, then up at the eighteen-inch hoses feeding hot air through the engines. "I can have something by the time these are up to temperature. It won't be pretty. No better than *maybe* able to save your lives."

"Good enough for me."

He was on the radio as he headed away toward the big equipment garage.

She stepped over to where the fuelie was rewinding her hose.

"I've got one more for you."

"Not anywhere to squeeze another drop in this bird, sister."

"I need two fuel drums and a hand crank. I'll burn the bladder tank first, then refill it from the drums. That's a hundred and ten gallons."

While the fuelie was rustling up the extra fuel, she called Ted on the radio. "Tell them that they're going to be lying down for the whole trip. Put them on air mattresses, not even stretchers. That will save us sixty pounds."

"Nine whole gallons of fuel. I feel so much better."

"Every ounce counts, Ted. Make sure you go to the bathroom before we takeoff and eat a light breakfast."

"Ha. Ha. Ha."

"Not kidding."

When he reached the plane, he eyed her two fuel drums and the hand pump. Then he looked down the runway to where a pair of snowcats were racing across the snow, one with a snowplow at the front and the other dragging a big roller.

His hood twisted to either side as if he was cricking his neck.

But he didn't say a word and she wanted to hug him for it.

14

TED ALMOST FORGOT HOW TO FLY.

It wasn't that they were overweight by an extra passenger and two drums of fuel. He trusted Jessica's mechanic's knowledge to make sure that was okay. Even knowing that she'd needed a longer runway just in case the snow was too sticky told him just how much math she'd done to make sure this was okay.

It wasn't that they now had two ailing patients to deliver alive across such an endless stretch of unforgiving ice. They were as comfortable as possible and their chances were tied to his own.

So what had changed since the flight down?

Holding Jessica through the night, and having the easiest sleep he'd managed in a long time. There was a rightness to her that he'd never felt before.

What was new, and giving him problems, was that he no longer had Jessica flying beside him. Their journey had transformed her from amazing to precious. If he'd crashed on the route down, it would have been awful. If he did it now, he'd have lost something so important that its loss was impossible to imagine.

He was also more alone on this flight. She was constantly out of her seat, checking on both patients. Jessica also went to the back to crank the pump and transfer the fuel from the drums to the bladder. And when the bladder had been drained, she rolled and squeezed it so tightly that not a cup of fuel could have remained.

That's when he appreciated the sixty pounds she'd saved by ditching the stretchers for air mattresses. There was no clearer signal of just how low their reserve was going to be.

"What's our leeway?" he asked one of the times she was back in the cockpit.

"With this headwind...not much. We landed at the Pole with fifteen percent fuel reserve, about 75 minutes. I'm hoping we still have fifteen minutes left by the time we land at Rothera. If not, we'll have to risk landing on the Larsen Ice Shelf and *Boris* will have to bring us some more fuel. At least we'll be back at sea level and our engines won't freeze."

"Fifteen minutes after seven-and-a-half hours..." He wished he could cut his tongue out. She was probably already stressing herself out to near her limits. If she even had limits. "Uh, sounds good. I can work with that."

As she rose to once more head back and check on the patients, she rested her hand briefly on his shoulder, squeezing it in thanks. Jessica Ryan did have limits. That was good to know, otherwise she might be just a little too terrifying.

15

SHE ACTUALLY CRIED WHEN THE SKIS TOUCHED DOWN AT Rothera. She couldn't help herself. It was just too much, too big. They all were safe.

But what about their moments on the ice? Had that been real? Or would it forever be a mere kiss at the South Pole? A kiss and sleeping in each others' arms. It was real. It had to be.

So why couldn't she trust it?

She kept the tears hidden.

Once the plane was secure and refueled, and the British medic had both patients in their tiny infirmary, she curled up alone in her bed and slept only fitfully.

She was barely conscious for the flight across the Drake Passage back to Punta Arenas. Ted had tried to start conversations, but she simply couldn't focus on anything beyond the weather and navigation.

At the airport, she was suddenly bereft.

One ambulance whisked away the stroke patient to the local hospital. The one losing his sight was hustled onto a flight headed back to the States.

Now it was just the two of them with *Natasha* the Twin Otter.

She'd finished unmounting the skis and tucking them away in the rear cabin, then she'd sat on the lip of the cargo deck unsure what to do with herself.

Ted came up and leaned on the doorjamb. Because the landing gear were tall on this plane, she looked slightly down at him. But he didn't face her. He faced out toward the water where the Straits of Magellan shimmered under the morning sun.

Sun! It was just past dawn in southern Chile. They'd survived the darkness of the Polar night inside the Antarctic Circle. She became aware of its warmth on her face.

It had been night for four days. Now that it was morning and she was completely out of sync with everything, including herself.

"I was thinking," Ted muttered as if to himself. "You've been a lot more places than I have."

"At least while Mom was alive. Though all our trips were in the US."

"Were they? Isn't that interesting."

She couldn't find the energy to ask why.

"You're going to need a swimsuit."

"You're going to need to get your head fixed. The

water here is probably a gazillionth of a degree above freezing."

"I was thinking," he continued as if she hadn't spoken. "We have this plane. We have to fly it halfway around the world to get it home."

"A third."

Again he ignored her comment. "I'm thinking there are probably a lot of interesting places between here and Montana. When was the last time you took a vacation?"

The day after she'd passed her A&P license exam. Mom had showed up with two prepacked knapsacks and a pair of tickets to Boulder, Colorado. A month later she'd been killed.

"That's what I thought," he spoke into her silence. "About the same for me." Then he fell silent.

A lot of places between Chile and Montana? And she needed a swimsuit? Between here and there were plenty of tropical beaches, cities she'd only ever heard of, places she'd never dreamed she'd get to on her own...

Travel for her had always been about "the two." Her and Mom.

But what if it was about her and someone else?

When she looked down at him, Ted was no longer studying the horizon. He was looking up at her.

He wanted to vacation with *her*? No, it was more than that. He wasn't suggesting some fling. He was

63

talking about trying each other on for size. Like finding just the right airplane for the job.

"For real?" It was all she could think to ask.

"For real. What do you think?"

What did she *think?* "I think it sounds absolutely one-hundred-percent glorious!"

Then Ted did the silliest thing, he started doing a little happy dance right there on the pavement beside their plane.

It was like her world had just opened up. The magic night of a mid-summer's eve had turned into a magnificently radiant day.

She hopped down from the cargo door to join him and together they danced a happy chicken-dance beneath the mid-winter sun.

DRONE (EXCERPT)

IF YOU ENJOYED THAT, YOU'LL LOVE
MIRANDA CHASE!

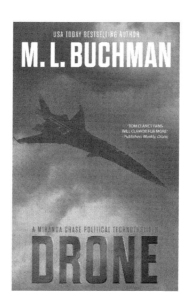

DRONE (EXCERPT)

Flight 630 at 37,000 feet
12 nautical miles north of
Santa Fe, New Mexico, USA

THE FLIGHT ATTENDANT STEPPED UP TO HER SEAT—4E—
which had never been her favorite on a 767-300. At
least the cabin setup was in the familiar 261-seat, 2-
class configuration, currently running at a seventy-
three percent load capacity with a standard crew of ten
and one ride-along FAA inspector in the cockpit jump
seat.

"Excuse me, are you Miranda Chase?"

She nodded.

The attendant made a face that she couldn't
interpret.

A frown? Did that indicate anger?

He turned away before she could consider the possibilities and, without another word, returned to his station at the front of the cabin.

Miranda once again straightened the emergency exit plan that the flight's vibrations kept shifting askew in its pocket.

This flight from yesterday's meeting at LAX to today's DC lunch meeting at the National Transportation Safety Board's headquarters departed so early that she'd decided to spend the night in the airline's executive lounge working on various aviation accident reports. She never slept on a flight and would have to catch up on her sleep tonight.

Miranda felt the shift as the plane turned into a modest five-degree bank to the left. The bright rays of dawn over the New Mexico desert shifted from the left-hand windows to the right side.

At due north, she heard the Rolls-Royce RB211 engines (quite a pleasant high tone compared to the Pratt & Whitney PW4000 that she always found unnerving) ease off ever so slightly, signaling a slow descent. The pilot was transitioning from an eastbound course that would be flown at an odd number of thousands of feet to a westbound one that must be flown at an even number.

The flight attendant then picked up the intercom phone and a loud squawk sounded through the cabin. Most people would be asleep and there were soft complaints and rustling down the length of the aircraft.

"We regret to inform you that there is an emergency on the ground. I repeat, there is nothing wrong with the plane. We are being routed back to Las Vegas, where we will disembark one passenger, refuel, and then continue our flight to DC. Our apologies for the inconvenience."

There were now shouts of complaint all up and down the aisle.

The flight attendant was staring straight at her as he slammed the intercom back into its cradle with significantly greater force than was required to seat it properly.

Oh. It was her they would be disembarking. That meant there was a crash in need of an NTSB investigator—a major one if they were flying back an hour in the wrong direction.

Thankfully, she always had her site kit with her.

For some reason, her seatmate was muttering something foul. Miranda ignored it and began to prepare herself.

Only the crash mattered.

She straightened the exit plan once more. It had shifted the other way with the changing harmonic from the RB2II engines.

———

Chengdu, Central China

AIR FORCE MAJOR WANG FAN EASED BACK ON THE joystick of the final prototype Shenyang J-31 jet—designed exclusively for the People's Liberation Army Air Force. In response, China's newest fighter jet leapt upward like a catapult's missile from the PLAAF base in the flatlands surrounding the towering city of Chengdu.

It felt as he'd just been grasped by Chen Mei-Li. Never had a woman made him feel like such a man.

———

Get Drone *and fly into a whole series of action and danger! Available at fine retailers everywhere.*

Drone

ABOUT THE AUTHOR

USA Today and Amazon #1 Bestseller M. L. "Matt" Buchman started writing on a flight south from Japan to ride his bicycle across the Australian Outback. Just part of a solo around-the-world trip that ultimately launched his writing career.

From the very beginning, his powerful female heroines insisted on putting character first, *then* a great adventure. He's since written over 60 action-adventure thrillers and military romantic suspense novels. And just for the fun of it: 100 short stories, and a fast-growing pile of read-by-author audiobooks.

Booklist says: "3X Top 10 of the Year." PW says: "Tom Clancy fans open to a strong female lead will clamor for more." His fans say: "I want more now...of everything." That his characters are even more insistent than his fans is a hoot.

As a 30-year project manager with a geophysics degree who has designed and built houses, flown and jumped out of planes, and solo-sailed a 50' ketch, he is awed by what is possible. More at: www.mlbuchman.com.

Other works by M. L. Buchman: *(* - also in audio)*

Action-Adventure Thrillers

Dead Chef
One Chef!
Two Chef!

Miranda Chase
Drone*
Thunderbolt*
Condor*
Ghostrider*
Raider*
Chinook*
Havoc*
White Top*

Romantic Suspense

Delta Force
Target Engaged*
Heart Strike*
Wild Justice*
Midnight Trust*

Firehawks
MAIN FLIGHT
Pure Heat
Full Blaze
Hot Point*
Flash of Fire*
Wild Fire
SMOKEJUMPERS
Wildfire at Dawn*
Wildfire at Larch Creek*
Wildfire on the Skagit*

The Night Stalkers
MAIN FLIGHT
The Night Is Mine
I Own the Dawn
Wait Until Dark
Take Over at Midnight

Light Up the Night
Bring On the Dusk
By Break of Day
AND THE NAVY
Christmas at Steel Beach
Christmas at Peleliu Cove
WHITE HOUSE HOLIDAY
Daniel's Christmas*
Frank's Independence Day*
Peter's Christmas*
Zachary's Christmas*
Roy's Independence Day*
Damien's Christmas*
5E
Target of the Heart
Target Lock on Love
Target of Mine
Target of One's Own

Shadow Force: Psi
At the Slightest Sound*
At the Quietest Word*
At the Merest Glance*
At the Clearest Sensation*

White House Protection Force
Off the Leash*
On Your Mark*
In the Weeds*

Contemporary Romance

Eagle Cove
Return to Eagle Cove
Recipe for Eagle Cove
Longing for Eagle Cove
Keepsake for Eagle Cove

Henderson's Ranch
Nathan's Big Sky*
Big Sky, Loyal Heart*
Big Sky Dog Whisperer*

Other works by M. L. Buchman:

Short Story Series by M. L. Buchman:

Printed in Great Britain
by Amazon